CW01081597

SPINE SHIVERS

RAINTREE IS AN IMPRINT OF CAPSTONE GLOBAL LIBRARY LIMITED, A COMPANY INCORPORATED IN
ENGLAND AND WALES HAVING ITS REGISTERED OFFICE AT 264 BANBURY ROAD, OXFORD, OX2 7DY –
REGISTERED COMPANY NUMBER: 6695582

WWW.RAINTREE.CO.UK
MYORDERS@RAINTREE.CO.UK

ORIGINATED BY CAPSTONE GLOBAL LIBRARY LTD
PRINTED AND BOUND IN INDIA

ISBN 978 1 4747 6139 0
22 21 20 19 18
10 9 8 7 6 5 4 3 2 1

BRITISH LIBRARY CATALOGUING IN PUBLICATION DATA
A FULL CATALOGUE RECORD FOR THIS BOOK IS AVAILABLE FROM THE BRITISH LIBRARY.

BIGFOOT ISLAND

BY J. A. DARKE

TEXT BY BRANDON TERRELL

ILLUSTRATED BY NEIL EVANS

raintree
a Capstone company — publishers for children

CONTENTS

CHAPTER ONE

Darius Robinson clutched his stomach and said, "Oh no. Not again." He staggered to the side of the ferry and threw up into the churning water of Lake Michigan. Again. It was the fourth time he'd been sick already. Darius didn't know how he still had anything left in his stomach.

The boat beneath his feet rocked from side to side, and he grabbed the cool metal rail to steady himself. He closed his eyes. This wasn't how his trip was supposed to start. The four Wilderness Warriors and their guide, Mr Horton, were about to spend three days camping and hiking on a small island in the middle of Lake Michigan. Darius had only been a Wilderness Warrior for a few months. When he joined the club, no one had mentioned that he'd be getting up before sunrise. Or that he'd be on a ferry in white-capped water for an hour. Or that he would get violently seasick. *Four* times.

And the trip had barely even begun!

Darius groaned and took a deep breath of the cool, misty morning air. He walked back to the ferry's cramped cabin, where the rest of the group sat, and collapsed onto one of the uncomfortable seats. They were faded red vinyl, weathered and torn in places, allowing the foam inside to spill out.

"You OK, D?" asked Jasmine Medina, a fellow Wilderness Warrior. Jasmine sat with one leg draped over the side of her chair. A large digital SLR camera was hanging around her neck.

Darius nodded. "I'll be fine."

Sammi Horton piped up from the other side of the cabin. "My dad calls that 'feeding the fishes'." Sammi had her head down, sketching in the notebook that Darius rarely saw her without, and didn't look up when she talked to him.

Darius tried to laugh, but his stomach lurched. He remembered a time when he was little and he'd got travel-sick being a passenger in the back of his parents' old car on a road trip. "Just keep your eyes on the horizon," his dad had suggested. So he'd stared out of the windscreen while they wove through the rocky, hilly terrain, and it had worked.

Darius tried that technique now. He tried to look out one of the cabin's windows but could only see the haze of early morning fog. "How much longer are we gonna be on this thing, anyway?" Darius asked no one in particular.

Alec Parnell, the last member of the Wilderness Warrior team, chimed in. "According to the Pine Island website, the ferry ride takes approximately one hour and ten minutes." He checked an enormous watch on his wrist. "We've been heading at a north-northeastern angle for about fifty minutes," he continued. "So I'd say we've got about twenty minutes left."

"Thanks," Darius muttered. Alec meant well but could be annoying. He was the type of kid who would point out logic flaws on a test, the kind who took the Wilderness Warrior pledge of "Expect the best, prepare for the worst" to heart. Even now, as the ferry shifted back and forth, Alec was casually unfolding a map of Pine Island.

In fact, as Darius glanced around the cabin, none of the other Wilderness Warriors looked as green and seasick as he was feeling.

"Why aren't you guys hurling your breakfast over the side like I am?" he asked.

It was Alec – of course – who answered. "I took dimenhydrinate when I woke up this morning," he said. Seeing the puzzled looks from the others, he added, "Motion sickness tablets. Duh."

Sammi shrugged. "I'm out on my dad's fishing boat all the time," she said. "This doesn't faze me a bit."

Jasmine, now positioning her camera out of an open window at the foggy sky and not paying attention to them at all, said nothing.

Alec rooted around in his backpack. "Here," he said, producing a packet of salty crackers. "Eat some of these."

He threw the crackers to Darius, who immediately broke them open. The dry, salty sting on his tongue was refreshing. Before too long, half of them were gone.

Darius pulled his own oversized backpack out from under his seat. They all seemed to have the same kind of pack, narrow with an extra zipped section for a sleeping bag. He unclipped his plastic water bottle from the side of the pack and took a long swallow of the iced water. When he'd filled it at home before leaving, his dad had reminded him, "Enjoy the ice while you can. For the next three days, you'll be filtering lake water to drink."

Darius had never really been camping before, except for the times he and his buddy Charlie set up a tent and slept in the back garden overnight. They'd run extension cables from the garage to power a fan, a small TV and a video game console so they could play *Splatterville 5* on it. Not exactly roughing it.

Pine Island was going to be something else entirely.

Footsteps thundered down the metal staircase leading into the cabin. Mr Horton, Sammi's dad and the group leader, was coming down to join them. An avid outdoor type, Mr Horton wore heavy boots, a pair of khaki shorts with pockets all over them, a bright blue Wilderness Warriors T-shirt and a floppy cap pulled low on his head.

"Greetings, Warriors!" he boomed, clapping his hands. "According to our illustrious captain upstairs, we're just moments away from making landfall. Now . . . who's ready for an adventure?" A grin broke through his heavy beard, revealing a set of perfect pearly white teeth.

"I am!" Sammi said, almost singing it.

Alec and Jasmine put up their hands.

Darius went to put up his hand, too, but his stomach made a disapproving sound.

Mr Horton noticed. "Uh-oh," he said, concerned. "Looks like someone is about to feed the fishes."

Sammi laughed. "See?"

Darius, who'd thought the salty crackers were helping, suddenly realized they were about to make an encore appearance. He stood up and bolted out of the cabin.

He had a brief moment to think, *Oh, the fog is clearing,* before he bent over the rail again.

As he wiped his mouth and straightened up, the sun began to appear through the morning haze. The dark water calmed, and a large, ominous shape began to materialize in the fog at the ship's bow.

From the unseen wheelhouse above the cabin, the ferry's captain sounded a foghorn. The three sharp blasts startled Darius, causing his heart to thunder, and set the deck below his feet to rumbling.

The fog parted, and the dark shape became clear. Pine Island, a cluster of rocks and trees jutting up into the sky, came into focus like a hidden treasure finally found. Or perhaps like a secret that wished to remain in the dark, now dragged out into the light.

CHAPTER TWO

With solid ground beneath his boots – well, his *dad's* boots, borrowed for the occasion and a size too big – Darius' stomach finally settled. He'd been the first to leap from the ferry to the dock and from the dock to the dirt path.

"I like your enthusiasm, Darius!" Mr Horton had shouted from the boat.

Darius gave him a thumbs-up, grateful to be on the island. For a few moments, it felt like he was still on the ferry. Phantom waves seemed to sway his body back and forth. But by the time the others had joined him, backpacks slung over their shoulders, the swaying was gone.

The Wilderness Warriors watched as the ferry captain waved goodbye and backed the boat away from Pine Island, heading for the mainland. He would not be returning until it was time for them to leave in three days.

"OK, everyone, stick together," Mr Horton said. "This place is filled with shadows. Wouldn't want anyone to get swallowed up by them!" He wiggled his fingers and gave a spooky laugh before chuckling at his own joke.

He was the only one laughing, though.

The path from the dock led up a small hill, where a sign carved from wood, with letters burned into it, read *Ranger Station*, along with an arrow pointing ahead.

The ranger station was hidden in a copse of towering pines, with shadows and a pocket of cool morning air surrounding it. Darius shuddered as they approached.

It was the end of summer, autumn and the new school year were looming ahead. Mr Horton had warned the Warriors that there wouldn't be many other hikers around, and so far they hadn't seen a single soul.

Mr Horton pulled open the ranger station's wooden door and motioned them inside. "After you, my brave Warriors!" he said.

Inside, the ranger station was not exactly what Darius had expected. He'd pictured a warm, rustic cabin. Instead, the place was filled with dead animals. Taxidermy busts of deer watched them from every wall. A giant moose head hung over the fireplace. Near the door, a plaque-mounted trout twisted as if jumping out of the water. An owl, wings outstretched, sat perched on a shelf above a glass counter filled with trinkets. Near the fireplace, surrounded by a pair of old patterned sofas and chairs, was a glass coffee table that held the curled-up remains of a taxidermied doe and three young fawns.

"This place is giving me the absolute heebie-jeebies," Darius whispered to Jasmine, who was studying a framed black-and-white photo.

A door behind the counter swung open, startling Darius. He stepped back, almost tripping over one of the overstuffed chairs. A woman emerged from the back room, striding out with a purpose and shutting the door behind her. A small sign on the door – Ranger's Office – swung back and forth.

"Greetings," the woman said. She was older, wiry, with skin like sandpaper and hair colour to match. She wore a khaki short-sleeve shirt with the word *Ranger* embroidered on it. The woman leaned both hands on the glass counter. As he approached, Darius noticed a thick, gnarled scar running the length of her left arm.

"My name is Ellis Malone," the woman said. "I'm the ranger here at Pine Island. Welcome."

"Thank you for having us," Mr Horton said. "We're all very excited about hiking around the island."

"And we're happy to have you. Now there are a few things I need to go over with you before you set out."

"All right," Mr Horton said. "Listen carefully, everyone."

"First off," Ellis Malone said. "This is our ranger station. There's also a small trading post just down the trail. We'll walk there in a short while. We *do* have a small selection of food and supplies at the post. But this is the only spot on the island with them, so best to stock up before you head out."

She motioned at a deer head with a large rack of antlers behind her left shoulder. "There are numerous forms of wildlife on the island, deer and moose especially."

"What about bears?" Alec chimed in. "I read in the travel guide that there have been black bear sightings on the mainland."

Ellis Malone shook her head. "No bears here that I'm aware of, unless they hopped on a ferry to get here," she said. "Even so, you'll want to bag and seal your food at night, and hang the bags in a nearby tree. Just to be safe."

"Comforting," Darius whispered under his breath.

Ellis Malone picked up a stack of maps, came around the corner, and began to hand them out. "Every campsite is equipped with an outhouse," she reported. Darius saw Jasmine's nose wrinkle briefly in disgust. "And every one is a short hike to the lake, where you will be able to gather water to filter, boil and drink."

She held out a map to Alec. "No thank you," Alec said, brandishing the map he was studying on the ferry. "I've got my own."

When she reached Darius, she held out the map with her left hand. Darius stared at the scar running the length of her arm. The scar was paler than the rest of her flesh.

"Is everything all right?" she asked.

Darius quickly snatched the map from her. "Yep," he said. "All good."

"Good." She put the remainder of the maps on the counter. "Now I'll show you to the trading post. Follow me."

"Gladly," Darius whispered, thankful to be leaving the creepy ranger station.

They walked single file down the path towards a second, smaller building. As they got near it, the front door opened. A bell jingled from the doorway, and three adults came out.

The man in the lead wore a ranger uniform similar to Ellis Malone's. A baseball cap was perched on his head.

"Hello, Mother," he said.

"Ben," said Ellis. She turned to the Warriors. "This is my son, Ben. He and I are the island caretakers. And these lovely people," she said, gesturing to the man and woman behind Ben, "are the Hendersons."

"Hi." The woman, whose blonde hair was tied up in pigtails, smiled and waved at the kids.

"Looks like our groups are the only hikers braving the island right now," Mr Henderson said.

"Yes," Ellis said.

"Well, then we'll see you down the dusty trail." Mr Henderson smiled and saluted the group. Then Ben led the Hendersons down the path, away from the trading post and ranger station.

The trading post was just as cramped as the station, but there was only one creepy taxidermy deer head on the wall. A sign around his neck read: *Don't forget your compass!* An arrow pointed down to a wicker basket filled with compasses.

Rows of short shelving units held essentials such as soap and toilet paper, batteries and snacks. A spinner rack of books and magazines sat in the corner, covered in dust and looking like no one had touched it in a long while.

The group of campers milled about. Jasmine spun the rack of books, while Sammi found a section of art supplies. Alec immediately stood by the door. "Not getting anything?" Mr Horton asked him.

"I've got everything I need," Alec replied.

Of course he does, Darius thought.

Darius bought a packet of trail mix and several sticks of beef jerky. The group had packed plenty of food, but he decided that he could never have enough snacks. He also took the deer head's advice and threw in a compass, seeing as he hadn't brought one with him. Then he waited while Sammi bought a set of coloured pencils and Jasmine stocked up on batteries.

"Everyone ready?" Mr Horton asked. The Warriors all nodded as they slipped out of the trading post and back out into the sunny morning. It was starting to get warm.

"Have fun, guys!" Ben Malone called out as he came back up the trail. Apparently he had guided the Hendersons for only a short distance before sending them off alone.

"We'll see you in three days, back here at the station," Ellis Malone said.

"See you then," Mr Horton replied. They shook hands.

Mr Horton led the group into the woods. "Off we go!" he shouted as the Wilderness Warriors began their hike around Pine Island.

CHAPTER THREE

Darius was sweaty and tired and wanted to sit down.

He was also a little embarrassed. He wasn't the most athletic kid, but he definitely didn't think the hike would wear him out as quickly as it had. Plus, it seemed like the other Warriors weren't bothered by the gruelling hike or by how hot the day had become.

They walked along a narrow path of hard-packed earth. Many hikers had walked the trail before; it was well worn. They wove through trees and brush, around large clusters of rocks and even under the thick,

rotting trunk of a fallen pine tree. Darius'
pack was cutting into his shoulders.

It must be almost lunchtime, he thought.
At lunch, he planned on ditching his coat
and using it to cushion his shoulders for
the afternoon hike.

Darius dug into his pocket and pulled
out the compass he'd bought at the trading
post. It was cheap, and he could see why.
The plastic cover was already cracked in
one place, and the needle pointed true
north for just a moment before twirling
around like it had a mind of its own.

"Weird," Darius whispered, tapping the
compass with a finger.

"I don't know why you bought that," Alec
said from behind Darius, "when we have
something like this."

Darius turned around to see Alec holding
up a device the size of a smartphone.
"Top of the line GPS system," Alec said. "I

know exactly how far we've travelled and how far we need to go before we reach camp."

An hour later, just as Darius' stomach began to loudly rumble, the group entered a clearing in the trees. Near them was a tall chain-link fence, three metres high at least. And in the centre was a square-shaped wooden structure that jutted up to the sky.

"What is that?" Jasmine asked.

"That," Mr Horton said, shielding his eyes from the sun with one hand and gazing up at the wooden structure, "is an abandoned ranger lookout tower. Must be at least twenty metres tall."

"It kind of looks like a tree house on stilts," Sammi said.

The tower had long posts on each of its four sides and a framework of criss-crossing support beams. In the middle of this was a set of wooden steps, and sitting at the top was a wide, covered platform with a railing around it.

"Can we climb it?" Jasmine asked, snapping a few photos of the tower. "I bet I can get some fantastic shots from up there."

Mr Horton shook his head. "I don't think they want us to go up there," he said.

Darius had to side with Jasmine, though. Despite being tired, he wanted to check it out. "It'd be a cool place to eat lunch," he suggested.

Jasmine nodded in the direction of a gate in the chain-link fence. It was open. "Technically, there's no sign saying to keep out," she said. "If the rangers didn't want us exploring the tower, the gate would be closed. Right?"

"Right," Darius agreed with a smile.

Mr Horton exhaled loudly. "OK," he said.

Jasmine dashed for the steps. "Yes!"

"No." Sammi shook her head. "You guys have a blast, but I'm keeping my feet on the ground." She slipped her backpack off and rested it against a flat boulder.

"Oh, come on," Darius said. "You have to join us. The view will be worth the hike."

"I am deathly afraid of heights," Sammi countered. "No, on second thought, I'm deathly afraid of *falling from* heights. So I'll eat my lunch down here." She sat on the boulder, unzipped her pack, and pulled out her water bottle, an apple and a plastic container of food.

"Suit yourself," Darius said.

"Are you sure you don't mind eating alone?" Mr Horton asked his daughter.

"One hundred per cent," Sammi said. "Go and enjoy the view."

And so, while Sammi made herself comfortable with her sketchbook and lunch, the rest of the group began to climb the abandoned tower's steps. It was harder than Darius had thought it would be, and by the time they reached the top, his leg muscles were burning.

"Totally worth it," he whispered as he dropped his pack and looked out from the tower's platform. The island's namesake pine trees grew thick and tall, making the view below look like a plush green carpet. The dark water of Lake Michigan stretched as far as Darius could see. He was equal parts astonished by the island's beauty and creeped out by its isolation.

"What a view," Jasmine said. She fearlessly leaned against the wooden railing, pointing her camera towards the ground. "Hey Sammi! Say cheese!" she shouted. Her voice echoed across the canopy of trees.

"Cheese!" a tiny voice cried back.

"All right, everyone," Mr Horton said, sitting cross-legged in the middle of the platform. "Let's have some lunch, shall we?"

The group sat in a circle, each getting their lunches out of their packs. Meals and food were carefully taken into account when packing for the trip. Each Warrior carried with them supplies for one dinner (mostly foods that could be boiled or didn't require refrigeration) and their own lunches.

Darius ate his lunch, finishing it off with a stick of beef jerky from the trading post.

Then he lay down on the platform, closing his eyes. The others ate in silence, in awe of the island's scope. The chirping of birds and the hum of insects drifted lazily around them.

I could get used to this, Darius thought as he let the peacefulness wash over him.

But that peacefulness was instantly shattered by a blood-curdling scream.

CHAPTER FOUR

"Sammi!"

Mr Horton leaped to his feet and thundered down the rickety wooden steps. The others scooped up their things as quickly as possible. Darius hefted his pack onto his shoulders and followed Alec down the steps. He could feel the whole tower sway as they quickly descended.

"Daddy!" Sammi had begun to climb the steps, but her fear of heights had kept her from getting too far. Mr Horton reached her in no time.

"Are you all right?" he asked.

Sammi nodded. "I'm fine," she said. "I just . . . I saw something."

"What do you mean?"

"There, in the woods." Sammi pointed towards the boulder where her sketchbook and lunch still sat. A thick piece of charcoal rested on the sketchbook.

"Was it an animal?" Mr Horton asked. Now convinced that Sammi was not injured, he took the last few steps and began to walk towards the trees.

"If it was, you most likely scared it off," Alec noted. "Animals are often way more scared of us than we are of them."

"I heard it breathing," Sammi said. "And, like, this low growl. It made the hair on my arms stand up." She ran her hands down her forearms, as if the terrified feeling had returned.

Mr Horton stepped to the edge of the

trees, looked around, then plunged into the undergrowth.

"Daddy!" Sammi tried to stop him, but Mr Horton was gone. Darius could hear him walking, the sound of snapping branches under his heavy footsteps. A moment later, he returned.

"Nothing," hc said, shaking his head. "However, I *did* see some trampled shrubs and grass. My guess is an animal was resting here, and we disturbed it." He motioned to the trail. "Let's get moving again. We have a few kilometres to go before we reach camp."

The Warriors fell back in line and continued their hike. Darius walked behind Sammi and often observed her gazing warily into the trees. Each rustle of leaves from a bird or a squirrel made her jump. Just watching her made Darius feel uneasy.

The group spoke very little as they hiked.

They reached the first campsite around dinner time. The site was a large patch of grass near the lake, with a handmade fire pit in the middle and a wooden outhouse just outside the camping area.

"I am *not* using that thing," Sammi said, disgusted.

"Let's set up tents before it gets dark," Mr Horton advised. There were three tents – one for the boys, one for the girls and one for Mr Horton. *Great,* Darius thought, *I have to share a tent with Alec.*

Once the tents were set up, Mr Horton assigned them tasks. "Darius, you and Jasmine gather wood for a fire. Alec and Sammi, gather water from the lake so we can start boiling water for dinner."

By the time the sun had set, the incident at the lookout tower was behind them. They enjoyed freeze-dried packets of chicken and rice cooked over a campfire for dinner, and while the fire was raging, they toasted marshmallows.

As the fire began to dwindle, Mr Horton said, "Looks like we need more firewood." He grabbed his bright LED lantern and headed off into the woods.

"Be careful!" Sammi called out. "And hurry back!"

Darius was licking the sticky marshmallow goo off his fingers when he spied Jasmine getting out of her tent with a book in her hand. She took a seat by the fire.

"What'cha reading?" Darius asked her.

Jasmine seemed startled by his question. Her eyes flickered to where Mr Horton had disappeared, then back to Darius. "Oh," she said nervously. "It's nothing."

"Looks like a book about the island," Alec said, not taking the hint that Jasmine didn't want to discuss it.

"Yeah," she said. "It is. I . . . I *borrowed* it from the trading post."

"Borrowed it?" Alec asked. "Or *stole* it?" He seemed appalled.

"I'm gonna take it back," Jasmine said defiantly. "But we were in a hurry, it was the only one there, and I didn't see a price tag on it."

"So you *stole* it?" Alec shook his head.

"Alec, seriously, just deal with it." Jasmine began to flick through the book's pages. "There's a load of cool photos of the island. Like, old black and whites."

While Jasmine read, Darius unfolded the map of the island Ellis had given him. He found the ranger station on the map and, in the flickering light of the bonfire, ran his finger along the trail they'd hiked that day. The lookout tower was there, and it appeared to be the only one on the island. Then he took out his compass and checked their position. The needle wavered but held at true north, out towards the lake.

"Guys?" Jasmine's voice cut through the silence. Darius looked up. In the orange glow of the fire, he could see her expression was serious. "I think I have an idea of what Sammi heard at the tower."

"What?" Sammi asked.

"I think . . . I think it could have been a Bigfoot."

There was a long moment of silence.

Then Darius burst out laughing. "You can't be serious."

"I *am*," Jasmine replied.

"Yeah, this island has a Bigfoot," Darius said, wiping tears from his eyes. He couldn't stop laughing. "He's just hanging out here with his buddies – aliens and mud creatures and evil clowns."

"I hate clowns," Alec said. "And Bigfoot isn't real."

"Exactly," Darius said.

"It's a cryptid," Alec explained.

He was met with silence.

"Cryptozoology is a pseudoscience that presumes the existence of creatures that real science can't prove. Bigfoot. Loch Ness Monster. The Chupacabra. Stuff like that."

"Well maybe you want to tell that to the lady in this old news story," Jasmine said, pointing at the book. "Check it out." The three other Warriors huddled around her, looking down at the pages of the Pine Island book.

"There's a story in here about a group of campers from a long time ago," Jasmine said. "Like, some article from a newspaper or something. Listen." Then, she began to read . . .

A trio of campers came to Pine Island, but only one would leave. The survivor, a young woman who wishes to remain anonymous, tells rangers and reporters her harrowing tale of a battle with a mythical beast. "It followed us across the island," she recounts. "It waited for the perfect moment, then took us one by one." As she began to describe the details of her friends' deaths, she was overcome with grief. It was several moments before she spoke again. "I was alone, having just found their bodies, when it attacked me."

When asked what the creature looked like, the woman described it as ". . . tall, so tall. Its coarse fur was matted with blood. At first, I thought it was a bear. Until I saw its hands. Large, padded hands with fingers and claws that reached out for me. It was like nothing I'd ever seen before."

How the woman escaped the massive beast remains unclear. The next thing she remembers is arriving at the ranger station in *the middle of the night, covered in blood. She was taken to a mainland hospital and treated for lacerations that required over one hundred stitches.*

The survivor, when prompted by authorities, provided the following sketch of the beast. "It was a Bigfoot," she says. "That's the best way to describe it." She paused here, as if to reconsider, but then nodded again. "Yes. A Bigfoot."

Is there any truth to her claim? Is the wild creature known as Bigfoot roaming around Pine Island? Perhaps the truth will never really be uncovered. (See image 34.3 on following page for sketch of beast.)

Jasmine stopped reading.

"Turn the page," Alec said. "I want to see what she drew."

Jasmine obliged.

What Darius saw made his blood run cold.

The charcoal sketch was like something out of a horror film. The creature was tall and gangly, with legs and feet that were too long. It reached out with clawed hands, and its huge, expressive eyes looked almost human.

"*Roar!*"

A giant shape leaped from the shadows.

The quartet of Wilderness Warriors shrieked. Sammi dug her fingers into Darius' arm. Alec stepped back and tripped over a log, falling on his backside.

Mr Horton laughed. "Whoa," he said. "Sorry, Warriors. I didn't think I'd scare you *that* much." He dropped his armload of wood next to the fire and helped Alec to his feet. "What are you reading?" he asked, pointing at the book. "Ghost stories?"

"Umm . . . kind of," Darius replied.

"Well, you all look a little worn out," Mr Horton said. "So maybe we should call it a night. I'll wait until the fire dies out, but you should head to your tents."

As the group began to go their separate ways, Mr Horton added, "Remember to seal up your food and hang it in a tree. Just in case."

After they'd tidied up the campsite, Darius and Alec slipped into their tent. "That story was nonsense," Alec whispered as they climbed into their sleeping bags. "Nothing more than an urban legend."

"Oh, totally," Darius agreed, but he had to almost push the words past his lips. Sure, he'd laughed at the first mention of Bigfoot. But why would the book contain a made-up story and article? It all seemed so . . . *real*.

Without discussing their reasons, the boys left one lantern on. Darius did his best to fall asleep, but each rustle from outside and every pop from the dying embers of the fire made his heart race. When he closed his eyes, he saw the charcoal sketch – the beast reaching out to him.

Like a tortoise hiding from danger, Darius slid his head down inside his sleeping bag and waited out the night.

* * *

He must have slept, because the next thing Darius knew, the haze of dawn was brightening the inside of the tent. There was movement outside, and he heard the unzipping of one of the other tents.

And then, clear as day, he heard Mr Horton say, "Oh no."

Darius sat up, quickly peeling himself from his sleeping bag. Beside him, Alec was still fast asleep. Darius crawled to the tent flap, unzipped it, and stuck his head out.

Mr Horton was stood in the middle of the campsite, hands on his hips, gazing around at the devastation.

The entire campsite had been ripped apart in the middle of the night.

CHAPTER FIVE

It was like a tornado had struck. Paper towels and toilet paper were strewn everywhere. The logs for the campfire had been scattered, and the ashes in the fire pit had been trampled. Some of their food, safely hung in trees the night before, was scattered around the site, the protective plastic bags torn to shreds.

"What kind of animal could have done this?" Alec asked.

After he'd seen the damage, Darius had woken Alec up. Mr Horton had woken the girls. The Wilderness Warriors now stood together in their pyjamas surveying the campsite.

"It looks like the work of a bear," Mr Horton said matter-of-factly.

Sammi shook her head. "That ranger said there weren't bears on the island, Dad. Remember?"

"Well, yes," Mr Horton said. "But unless moose have found a way to tear open plastic bags of food, or have teamed up with raccoons in a plot for world domination, this is the work of a bear."

"It could have been a Sas–" Jasmine began.

"What about those other campers? The Hendersons?" Darius interrupted her. He didn't want to think about where she was heading with her suggestion.

"They seemed like very nice people," Alec said. "This would be a terrible prank to pull."

"Plus, we haven't seen them since they left the ranger station," Sammi added. "For all we know, they could be on the other side of the island."

"Let's just clean it up as best we can and be on our way," Mr Horton said. He already had a mound of paper towels in his hands and was shoving them into a pocket of his backpack.

The group cleaned in silence, packing their things and taking stock of their food. Thankfully, they still had enough to last them the whole trip. But they'd need to be careful with it. When the site was clear of damage, they took down their tents and prepared to leave. Alec studied his map. "The trail today is only five kilometres long," he said. "Much of it is along the shoreline."

When they were about to leave, Mr Horton found a long fallen branch to use as a walking stick. It was just thick enough for him to stick a fluttering roll of toilet paper on top of it. "Hark! Onwards, Wilderness Warriors!" he shouted, pointing the toilet paper–topped stick in the direction of the hiking trail. This bit of silliness was just what the group needed. They laughed, shaking their heads at Mr Horton.

"Your dad is weird," Darius said to Sammi.

"Yep," she said. "He's pretty much the best."

The group began down the trail. Alec was right – much of their path followed the shoreline, occasionally curving back up into the shade of the trees. It was growing hot again, the sun pressing down on them, but Darius spied dark clouds in the distance.

"Is it supposed to rain?" he asked.

Mr Horton followed his gaze. "Looks like it's still a little way off," he said. "But tonight may be a wet one."

"Lovely," Jasmine said. She snapped a photo of the horizon and the ominous clouds.

It was mid-afternoon when the group

reached a cliff cut into the side of the island. It was nothing treacherous, but there were a few spots where Darius found himself climbing loose stones and stepping from boulder to boulder.

As they reached the brow of the cliff, Mr Horton pointed his toilet paper walking stick to the water below. "Look," he said.

Down on the shoreline, wading through the shallows of the lake, were two enormous moose. They lumbered along, drinking from the lake, lifting their heads and majestic antlers as they checked their surroundings. Darius had never seen moose in real life. Well, except for the taxidermied one hanging in the ranger station.

"I want to get a closer look," Jasmine said. She was eyeing the animals through her camera lens.

"Be careful," Mr Horton warned Jasmine as she began to move along the clifftop.

One step. Then another. A slope to her right dropped down three metres or so, ending near the edge of the treeline.

As Jasmine started to crouch, aiming her camera at the moose, her right foot stepped on loose gravel. Darius saw it in slow motion, but it was too late to cry out a warning.

Jasmine's foot slipped out from under her. She tried to catch herself but fell back. Her hands still clutched her camera as she landed hard and began to slide down the rocky face.

"Help!" she cried out as she tumbled down.

"Jasmine!" Mr Horton had already dropped his walking stick and was rushing forward as she came to a sudden stop at the bottom of the embankment. He was careful to avoid the loose stones as he slowly found his way down the slope.

Darius followed. Of course, Mr Horton could probably handle it on his own, but

Darius couldn't just stand there and *not* help.

When they reached Jasmine, Darius could see bright crimson blood covering her bare right knee. It ran in streaks down her calf and pooled in her sock.

"Jasmine, are you OK?" Mr Horton asked.

"Yeah, I'm fine," she answered with a sharp intake of breath.

Mr Horton examined her leg and got her to straighten it for him. She gritted her teeth through the pain, choosing to focus her attention on her camera. "I think I cracked my lens, though."

Sure enough, a thin spiderweb of a crack ran the length of the glass lens. Jasmine shouted, "Stupid moose!" Her voice bounced through the boulders and echoed across the cliffs.

"Let me get your knee patched up," Mr Horton said. He shrugged off his pack and took out a first-aid kit.

As Mr Horton cleaned Jasmine's scrapes and wrapped her knee in gauze and bandages, Darius caught something bright and colourful out of the corner of his eye. At first, he thought he was seeing things in the shrubs. But when he took a couple of steps towards it, he saw it more clearly.

"Is that a backpack?" he asked himself.

Darius pushed aside the thick shrubs, branches scratching his hands and arms. It *was* a backpack. Bright yellow and blue.

"Guys!" he shouted. "Check it out!"

He pulled the pack from its hiding spot. On the bottom, Darius could see flecks of what looked like dried mud, or maybe even blood. There was a long gash along one side.

Sewn onto one of the pockets was a patch that read: Property of Fred Henderson.

"Mr Horton?" Darius held up the pack, his hands shaking a bit.

Mr Horton's face lost colour, and he quickly

helped Jasmine to her feet. "Come along," he told them as he draped Jasmine's arm over his shoulder for support. "And bring the pack with you, Darius."

At the top of the cliffside, Darius dropped the pack. "It says it belongs to Mr Henderson," he said as the Warriors gathered around it. Jasmine sat on a boulder nearby, her injured leg outstretched. She was fussing with her camera again.

"Henderson is a very common name," Mr Horton said. He unzipped the pack and began to remove its contents for clues. "There's a chance another hiker lost it earlier this summer."

Darius could hear the concern in Mr Horton's voice.

The contents of the pack made the answer quite obvious. Plastic bags contained food that hadn't been opened. A light on the walkie-talkie Mr Horton clicked on still glowed red, its battery working fine. And a wallet contained an ID and family photos that showed a smiling Mr Henderson, his wife and a pair of dogs.

"He must be worried sick about this," Mr Horton said. "We'll take the pack with us, make sure he gets it back."

"You think he just . . . *lost* it?" Alec asked. "It seems unlikely that he wouldn't be nearby searching for it."

Darius had an idea. He picked up the walkie-talkie and flicked it on. "Hello?" he said. "Can anybody hear me?"

Silence was his answer.

Darius tried again. "Mr and Mrs Henderson? Can you hear me? We have your pack at the cliffside. We're hiking to . . ."

He glanced over at Alec, who whispered, "Campsite B."

"Campsite B," Darius repeated into the walkie-talkie.

He waited for a response. It never came. Darius clipped the walkie-talkie to his belt in case the Hendersons replied while they were hiking.

Mr Horton repacked Mr Henderson's belongings and zipped the backpack closed. As he stood up, Darius heard a clatter behind him on the rocks. He spun around to see Jasmine, eyes wide, mouth open. Her camera, her pride and joy, lay on the ground in front of her.

With one trembling finger, she pointed at the camera. "It was here," she whispered. "It's following us."

"What is?" Mr Horton asked.

"Bigfoot." Her voice caught in the wind and was nearly drowned out. Darius heard her, though.

They all did.

CHAPTER SIX

"I can't see it," Alec said, putting his nose almost directly on the camera's viewscreen and peering intently.

"We're not safe here," Jasmine said, looking at the trees. Her gaze travelled back and forth so much it was making Darius dizzy just watching her.

"Let me have a look," Darius said, holding out his hand.

Alec passed the camera to him. He toggled through the images on the camera's small viewscreen.

Horizon. Moose. Moose. Sky. Blue blur. Green blur. *Jasmine must have snapped photos while she was falling*, Darius thought.

But then he found two that *were* in focus, shots where the camera was tilted at a weird angle. The trees looked like they were leaning over, diagonal lines across the screen. A patch of sunlight filtered through the trees.

And there, in the background of the photo, was a hulking shadow looking out from behind a tree trunk.

A wave of goosebumps coursed along Darius' arms, up his back and made the hair on the nape of his neck stand at attention.

"There." He pointed to the shadow.

Sammi and Alec peered at the viewscreen, and Sammi let out a sharp gasp.

"OK!" Mr Horton suddenly shouted. "That. Is. *Enough*." He strode over, angrily tore the camera from Darius' hands, and shoved it into Jasmine's backpack. "I've had enough of this talk about some make-believe monster in the woods. You're searching for things that just *don't exist*. This isn't a fairy tale. We have one Warrior badly hurt, and a man is missing his belongings."

Mr Horton turned to face the lake. He placed his hands on his hips, took deep breaths, and tried to collect himself. When he turned back to the group, his voice was calmer. "Our campsite for the night is nearby. We'll hunker down there and ride out whatever storm is coming. In the morning, we'll head back to the ranger station."

"We're leaving early?" Jasmine asked, sounding relieved.

"Yes," Mr Horton said. "We are. Now let's go." He took the roll of toilet paper off of his walking stick – his humour officially gone – and passed the branch to Jasmine.

"I can walk," she told him.

"I know," he replied. "But this will help."

The Warriors continued down the trail. Jasmine hiked at the front, just behind Mr Horton. Then Alec, followed by Sammi. Darius brought up the rear. They hiked in silence. It was much too quiet in the woods, as if even the air itself had up and vanished.

I can't hear any birds, Darius thought. *No birds. No insects. No squirrels or chipmunks.* He guessed the animals could sense the impending storm and had already found shelter for the night.

Occasionally during the hike, Darius would take out the walkie-talkie, thumb the button and whisper, "Hello?" into it.

He never got a response.

Campsite B was almost identical to the first one, except now they were nestled in the centre of a circle of pines that stretched towards the darkening sky. They moved quickly to set up their tents, placing them closer together now.

The first raindrops fell as Darius and Alec tied the flysheet over the top of their tent. They ducked inside. Before long, the wind shifted from a calm breeze to a howling force. The gusts bent the pine branches and hissed through their needles. Rain poured down, hammering the side of the tent.

The boys ate inside their tent, by lantern light. Darius finished the last of his jerky, and Alec ate trail mix. Occasionally, when the wind would momentarily die down, Mr Horton would slip out of his tent and kneel in front of theirs. "Everything OK in here?" he'd ask, his hat wet and drooping, his boots coated in mud.

Darius and Alec would give him thumbs-ups, and he'd proceed to the girls' tent to ask the same thing.

Alec fell asleep with his book splayed open on his chest, while Darius continued to toss and turn. It was closing on midnight when Darius finally began to drift off to sleep.

It was in this soft area, the one between wakefulness and dreamland, that Darius heard the crackle of static. "H-h-help," a woman's voice whispered. "H-h-help me. Please."

Darius opened his eyes. Was he hearing things? *What was that?*

The walkie-talkie rested on the ground between the boys. As Darius glanced down at it, he could have sworn he saw its red light flicker, like someone was trying to speak to them.

He snatched it up. "Hello?" he hissed into the walkie-talkie. He was suddenly alert. "Hello?" he said, louder.

"What's going on?" Alec mumbled. He sat up and wiped sleep from the corner of one eye.

"Did someone say 'help'?" Darius asked into the walkie-talkie.

Nothing.

Outside, the rain continued to pour down.

"Come on," Darius muttered. "Hello?!"

But the walkie-talkie just crackled and hummed.

"What did you hear?" Alec asked.

"Someone calling for help," Darius said. "A woman. She sounded scared."

"Are you sure you didn't dream it?"

"Yes, I'm sure." But *was* he? The more Darius thought about it, the more he started to wonder if he really *had* heard the woman on the walkie-talkie. Maybe Alec was right. Maybe he'd just dreamed it all.

"Hello?" he tried one last time.

When there was no answer, Darius decided it must have been in his imagination. He laid back in his sleeping bag, put the walkie-talkie on his chest, and closed his eyes. Sleep did not find him again for a long time that night.

When he did wake up, the first thing he noticed was the silence. The rain had stopped, but the air inside the tent still felt damp and cool. The sun was not up yet, and the secluded campsite was still shrouded in darkness.

Darius wanted to sleep again – sleep until this whole weird camping trip was nothing but a dream. His bladder, however, had other ideas.

Darius crawled to the edge of the tent, slipped on his boots, and ducked out of the tent. The outhouse was not far away. He'd just have to tiptoe across the campsite, past the girls' tent, and past–

"Mr Horton?"

The flap to Mr Horton's tent was unzipped and lying trampled and caked with mud on the ground.

And Mr Horton wasn't there!

CHAPTER SEVEN

"Hello! Mr Horton?"

Darius' calls woke the rest of the Warriors, and soon they were all standing outside their tents, hugging themselves for warmth.

"Where's Daddy?" Sammi asked, beginning to sound panicked.

"I'm sure he just went out for more firewood or something," Alec said. "Or to use the outhouse."

"The outhouse with the door wide open?" Sammi fired back. Sure enough, the door of the outhouse hung ajar. Mr Horton was nowhere near it.

"Mr Horton!" Darius called at the top of his voice.

"There's no way he would have left his tent this way." Sammi was studying the messy, muddy flap of her father's tent. She crouched down, looked inside, and shook her head. "His stuff is still here."

Darius gazed into the shadowy forest, looking for movement, for a flash of colour. It made no sense. There was no way the Warriors' leader would just . . . *leave* them.

"Guys, look at this." Jasmine hobbled to the side of Mr Horton's tent. A giant puddle of wet mud pooled there, just on the edge of the forest. Right in the middle of it was what looked like . . .

"A footprint?" Darius was amazed. It wasn't like any footprint he'd ever seen before, not human *or* animal, but a combination of both. It was huge, lean and deep, with toes and not the pads of an animal paw. And it was heading right into the trees.

Darius walked into the forest, following the footprint's direction. There were more footprints in a row. And next to them was a trail of smeared dirt and broken twigs.

"Whatever it was, it looks like it was dragging something," Darius said.

"Or some*one*," Alec added.

"Daddy!" Sammi crashed through the forest, shoving past Darius. She was panicked, her chest heaving with ragged breath. "Daddy!"

"Sammi, wait!" Darius caught up with her quickly, snagging her arm and dragging her to a stop.

"Let *go* of me!" she shouted, pulling away from him.

Darius held tight. "Stop," he said, trying not to sound as frantic as he was feeling. "We can't just rush off after him."

"But he may be in trouble!"

"I know. But if you just run off like that, we'll all get lost."

"Darius." Sammi's voice was surprisingly calm. "It's my dad."

"Let's hurry up, get as much of our stuff as we can, and *then* follow the trail. OK?"

Darius yelled back to Alec and Jasmine, telling them to start gathering things they needed. "Move quick," he said. "We're going to follow whatever left those footprints, and hopefully we'll find Mr Horton. If not, we're heading back to the ranger station."

"Wait," Jasmine said. "We're gonna *go after* the Bigfoot?"

Darius shook his head. "We're going after Mr Horton. And whatever gets in our way."

Even though they scrambled to tear down their tents, pack them up and cram the rest of their belongings into their packs, it felt like it was taking an eternity. As they worked, Darius kept hoping that Mr Horton would return and that it would all be some sort of misunderstanding.

But he didn't.

And it wasn't.

They were on their own.

When they were prepared to leave, Darius took a deep breath and one last look at the campsite and the enormous footprint in the mud. Then he led the way, plunging into the woods, following the trail left by the enormous creature.

The hike was tedious, with Jasmine's injury slowing them down. Sammi was particularly frustrated, urging them on even though Jasmine couldn't move quickly. They walked outside the hiking path, instead following the footsteps and line of smeared grass and mud alongside it.

Eventually, though, the trail grew fainter and fainter.

Then it disappeared completely.

"Daddy!" Sammi cried.

"Alec, where are we?" Darius asked. He was hungry and tired. With the thick clouds overhead, he couldn't tell the time. Alec, who'd been carrying Mr Henderson's pack as well as his own, fumbled with both until he got his map out. Then he tried to find their location.

"I . . . I don't know," he admitted. "We've been walking north-west, I think." He pulled out his GPS to check their coordinates. His brow furrowed, and he smacked the device a couple of times. "Stupid thing broke," he muttered.

They tried swapping out batteries, but still, the GPS system's screen remained black.

"Great," Jasmine said. She sat heavily on a fallen tree trunk, massaging her wounded leg. The bandages around her knee were caked with dried blood, but Darius could see new, dark crimson blossoming around the outside of it. A thin trickle escaped the bandage and ran down her leg.

"Wait a second," Darius whispered. He reached into his pocket and drew out the cheap, plastic compass he'd bought at the ranger station. "Thanks for the advice, dead deer," he said, remembering the sign dangling from the taxidermy deer. *Don't forget your compass!*

Darius threw the compass to Alec. "See if you can get us back on track." Then he unclipped the walkie-talkie from his belt and tried to reach the Hendersons. "Is anybody there?" he asked.

Maybe they're on another channel, he suddenly thought. *Or maybe I can reach the ranger station.* So he clicked through the dial, asking the same three words on each channel. "Is anybody there?"

No one replied.

"Just gonna say it," Darius announced loudly. "Not a fan of camping anymore. Pretty sure I'm not the only one, either."

This drew a smirk from Jasmine. "Yeah, not a fan," she added.

"I feel so woefully unprepared for what we're dealing with," Alec said as he examined the map and held Darius' compass.

Sammi scanned the forest and said nothing.

Finally, Alec pointed up a slight incline. "The trail should be in that direction," he said. He wiggled the compass. "I think."

"It's our best bet," Darius said. "Let's go."

Darius helped Jasmine to her feet and passed her the walking stick. Then he set off in the direction Alec had suggested.

Trees. All they saw was trees. On all sides, every direction they turned. Darius tried not to let it overwhelm him, because the minute he thought about it, his chest started to tighten, like someone had placed a heavy stone on it. They were lost, they didn't have an adult with them, and worst of all, something was hiding in the woods, hunting them.

"Guys!" Alec said finally, jumping up and down. "I see it! I see the trail!"

It must have been close to dinner time, because the cloud cover was getting darker. Darius quickened his pace, until he broke out of the forest – and onto the path. The actual, honest-to-goodness path!

"We found it!" He high-fived Alec and gave Jasmine a quick hug. Sammi, who had been looking more and more upset, did not seem very happy to have found the trail.

"We'll get back to the ranger station," Darius explained, "and Ellis Malone will have a search party out in no time to find your dad." He took Sammi's hand and squeezed it.

They broke out food then and ate as they

walked. Now that they were moving in the right direction, their pace was more confident. When it grew dark, they each took out a torch. The lights cut brilliant beams across the woods, making shadows jump and move.

A droplet of rain landed on Darius' forehead. *Oh no*, he thought. *Please don't start pouring again.*

As if on cue, a flash of lightning split the sky in half. For a split second, the forest was lit up as if it was day. Darius' heart raced and clattered against his chest.

Crack-a-BOOM!

Thunder followed close behind, meaning the storm was near.

"I don't think we're gonna make it back to the ranger station," Darius said. "We need to find our first campsite and stay there for the night."

"It should be close," Alec said. He was still

holding his map, cradling his torch between his chin and shoulder. Raindrops struck the map.

From behind them on the path, Darius heard the sound of footsteps and the huffing of breath. *No way*, he thought. *Has Mr Horton found us?*

"You guys hear that?" he asked, turning to search for the source of the footsteps.

Sammi perked up. "Daddy!" she shouted. "Daddy, is that you?"

She trained her torch beam on the path behind them. At the same time, lightning cracked above them . . . and illuminated a snarling, angry beast. It loped towards them with outstretched arms.

CHAPTER EIGHT

A peal of thunder shook the forest floor and nearly drowned out the Wilderness Warriors' screams. Darius felt his feet turn to cement. The monster was thirty metres away. Then twenty. Ten.

This can't be real, Darius told himself. *There's no such thing as Bigfoot.*

But the slobbering, lumbering beast could be nothing else. It was fighting its way through the woods towards the group of scared, scrambling kids. It was real, it was angry, and if they didn't run, it would kill them all.

"Move!" Darius shouted.

Four beams of light spun like crazed searchlights as the Wilderness Warriors tried to escape. Darius ran headlong into Sammi, who dropped her torch. Its beam glimmered in the Bigfoot's red, beady eyes. Darius grabbed hold of her top, turned her, and shoved her in the opposite direction.

The others followed. Alec draped Jasmine's arm around his shoulder, and the two moved as one. They hobbled together, and for a split second, looked like they were running a terrifying three-legged race.

"Go! Go!" He urged them. As if their situation wasn't bad enough, heavy, cold raindrops began to fall, the kind that stung when they struck.

Behind them, the beast stopped. It huffed and snatched something off the ground.

"Mr Henderson's pack," Alec said, winded. "I dropped it . . . hoping . . . all his food would . . . slow it down."

"Good thinking," Darius said.

Through the dim light, Darius saw the Bigfoot rip Mr Henderson's backpack open, spilling his things along the path. It stooped down to examine them.

They climbed a hill and ran down the other side, losing sight of the Bigfoot behind them. They slipped and slid down the sloppy trail. Sammi fell hard, sliding most of the way down the slope on her backside and standing up with a leg caked in mud.

Darius heard the monster roar, then the sound of splitting wood, as if the angry monster had snapped a tree in two. Its thunderous steps followed.

I don't wanna be the next thing it snaps, Darius thought.

Finally, as lightning flashed again, Darius spied a familiar clearing ahead. They had reached the first campsite. But as they staggered into the opening, he suddenly wondered where they could hide.

Jasmine had the answer.

"There!" She pointed to the wooden outhouse.

There was no time to be grossed out.

Alec helped Jasmine step up into the outhouse. Then Darius shepherded Sammi and Alec in before joining them.

He closed the door tight. A small latch acted as the outhouse's lock. Darius quickly latched it, feeling ridiculous as he did. A flimsy metal lock was the only thing standing between a monstrous beast and four terrified teens.

No one moved. Their torch beams illuminated the cramped confines. In the corner of the outhouse, a spider had woven an intricate web. Several insects wrapped in spider silk stuck to the web. The stench in the outhouse was beyond disgusting, but

Darius did his best to breathe through his mouth. He lifted the collar of his wet top up over his nose and mouth. It helped, but only a little.

"Lights off," he whispered.

The remaining three torches winked off, and pitch blackness blanketed them.

Darius tried to control his breathing. He could hear the others attempting to do the same. But it was hard. Impossible. His teeth clacked together.

They were so tightly packed into the outhouse, Darius could feel every shift and turn. He was pressed close to Sammi, who huddled next to Jasmine.

As his eyes adjusted to the dark, Darius could see thin vertical gaps in the slats of wood. Through these, he could peer out and glimpse a small part of the campsite.

Outside, the rain continued. They waited, five minutes . . . ten . . . fifteen.

Finally, Jasmine shifted and whispered, "Do you think–?"

Her question was answered before she'd even finished asking it. A roar of anger came from outside. Darius, one eye peering through a slat, saw the great, hulking beast walk towards the campsite. Its arms were freakishly long, its fur matted. It was odd how *human* it looked.

The Bigfoot trudged closer. Darius could hear it breathing, huffing like an ape, searching for their scent. Darius hoped the foul stench of the outhouse masked them enough.

The monster prowled the campsite. It didn't seem to recognize they were close. With a snarl, the Bigfoot struck his chest with one fist, then began to lope off into the forest.

Darius kept his eye to the slat, expecting the beast to return. His muscles screamed in agony. They'd been cramped in the outhouse for an hour at the very least.

Finally he unlocked the outhouse door and slowly opened it. "I think the coast is clear," he whispered.

The rain was nothing but a light sprinkle now – the kind of cold drizzle that slowly seeps in and chills to the bone.

Sammi and Alec emerged from the outhouse. Darius helped Jasmine, who leaned heavily on the walking stick.

"What do we do now?" Alec murmured.

"We keep moving," Darius replied. "We know the direction of the ranger station now. We stay quiet and walk as fast as we can."

"Right," Alec said. "Stay quiet."

Darius led the way, taking careful steps down the trail, trying to move as silently as possible. One hill. Then another. They walked in darkness, afraid to turn on their torches. Lightning pulsed in the distance. The first wave of the storm had passed.

But another was on the way.

Darius took Jasmine's hand as they descended a short, rocky hill. At the bottom, as they were about to move on, the red light on the walkie-talkie clipped to Darius' waist bloomed brightly.

"H-hello?" a tinny, distant voice hissed from the walkie-talkie.

Darius felt like a jolt of electricity had buzzed through him. In the still forest, the voice on the walkie-talkie sounded like it was coming from a megaphone.

So he *had* heard a voice on the walkie-talkie the night before! It wasn't his imagination after all. Quickly, Darius unclipped the walkie-talkie and cranked the volume down.

"Help . . ." the woman said. "There was . . . a *monster*. . . . It took us."

Darius thumbed the walkie-talkie and whispered, "We're going for help. If you can hear me, we're heading back to the ranger station for help."

Behind and to the right of the Warriors, Darius heard a snort and snarl. *The Bigfoot!*

It had heard them.

It was coming back for them.

"Hurry!" The voice over the walkie-talkie began to sob. "Hurry . . ."

"We've got to go," Alec said. He was staring into the woods.

Darius began to hurry along the trail again, leading the others. The sound had disappeared. *Maybe we lost it*, he thought hopefully.

Darius was moving at almost a full run before he realized how fast he was going. There was no way Jasmine could keep up with his pace. He glanced back over his shoulder to see where the others were.

"Oof!"

Darius slammed into something hard, bringing him to a sudden, staggering stop. The walkie-talkie flew from his hand, landing in the mud. Darius turned his head back to see what he had struck.

And he came face to face with the Bigfoot!

CHAPTER NINE

The monster reached out, took Darius in its vice-like grip, and lifted him off the ground. Darius, arms pinned to his sides, could do nothing as the Bigfoot held him up and examined him. It sniffed, snorted and peered at him with beady eyes. Hot breath that smelled like rotting meat washed over Darius, making him gag. He did his best to hold his breath.

"Please . . ." Darius managed to squeeze the word past his lips as the Bigfoot tightened its grip on him. It made Darius think of the splintering tree, how his own bones were more fragile. "Don't . . . hurt me. . . ."

The Bigfoot's expression remained unchanged. It wasn't going to listen to terrified pleas.

It was going to kill him.

Darius closed his eyes. He couldn't look at the beast any longer.

A brief, sudden blaze of light filled the forest. The Bigfoot howled, and Darius could feel its grip on him loosen. He wriggled free and fell to the muddy earth.

"You like that?" he heard Jasmine shout.

Darius pulled himself to his knees as a second burst of light made the monster roar again. *That isn't lightning*, he thought as he wiped his eyes with the wet sleeve of his jacket, *but what is it?*

Darius looked up and saw the monster with a hand over its face. Jasmine stood before it, her camera held high.

"My lens may be broken," she shouted, "but my flash is fine!"

She snapped another photo, and the flash unleashed a third blast of light. Darius rose to his feet as the Bigfoot swiped blindly at Jasmine. She ducked, but the monster's hand connected with the camera, knocking it away from her and shattering it on the ground.

Darius waved Sammi over to him. "Keep running!" he cried out, his voice hoarse and scratchy.

Blinking furiously, the Bigfoot advanced on Jasmine, who remained rooted in place after the monster's stunning attack.

Alec, however, was not frozen. He picked up the walking stick Jasmine had dropped and wielded it like a baseball bat.

"Run," he said to Jasmine.

She did her best, finally finding her legs

and hobbling towards Darius. Alec gripped the stick and swung at the monster. He struck the beast solidly across the chest. The stick splintered, and the monster stumbled backwards. It tripped on a exposed root and, like a falling tree, crashed to the forest floor.

The Wilderness Warriors didn't hesitate. They ran headlong down the trail. Even Jasmine, whose leg must have been absolutely killing her, was keeping up the pace. Darius didn't know how they'd be able to make it to the ranger station, though. It was still so far away.

Darius could hear the Bigfoot howling in agony behind them. But then the howl transformed into something that sounded to Darius like a cry for help.

A moment later, a second cry echoed through the forest.

Then a third.

A fourth.

They were coming from all around the island.

"There's more of them," Darius said.

There was nothing they could do but continue to run. Branches clawed at their arms and faces as the group passed a thick thicket of trees and shrubs. Gnarled roots caught Alec, and he tripped hard, landing on his left arm and crying out in pain.

Darius skidded to a stop, and he and Jasmine helped Alec to his feet. Alec winced and clutched his arm.

"You gonna be OK?" Darius asked.

"We are running around an island filled with Bigfoots," Alec replied. "I doubt it."

"Yeah, when the Wilderness Warriors said, 'Expect the best, prepare for the worst', this isn't exactly what they had in mind, is it?" Darius said.

Through his wincing, Alec managed to chuckle.

The wind began to whip again, bending the trees around them. When lightning streaked across the sky, Darius looked up.

Relief washed over him.

The lightning had revealed a giant shape against the black sky ahead of them.

The lookout tower!

It was a long shot, but maybe, just *maybe*, the Bigfoot wouldn't be able to detect them if they climbed to the top of the tower. Of course, they could also be trapping themselves high off the ground with zero chance to escape. Either way, their hope of surviving the night was slim. If they climbed the tower, at least they had a chance. Darius pointed to it. "We're close!" he shouted.

They reached the clearing that led to the tower and ran towards the gate.

Before reaching it, though, Darius came to a stuttering stop in the mud. The others nearly collided with him. "Look," he said. "The gate is closed now!" Sure enough, the gate that was open when they'd explored the area before was now shut tight. A thick chain was looped around it.

"It's locked!" Jasmine said with panic in her voice.

Darius cursed under his breath. Leading with his shoulder, he smashed into the gate. It budged, not a lot, but enough to reveal a narrow gap between the fence and the gate.

"Do you think we can squeeze through it?" Jasmine asked.

"We have to," Darius replied.

"Are you crazy?" Sammi burst out. She hadn't spoken for so long, Darius was shocked by the sound of her voice. She pointed at the tower. "You want to go *up there*? In the middle of a storm?"

"What other option do we have?" Darius asked.

Sammi glanced up at the tower, then back at the forest. Another round of cries from the pack of Bigfoots convinced her. "Fine," she muttered.

They took off their backpacks and lobbed them over the fence. Then, one by one, they squeezed through the slim gap. Darius pushed against the gate while Jasmine went through. Sammi silently followed. Alec, the largest of the group, barely fit. When he was through, he pulled the gate towards him so Darius could enter.

Darius sucked in his stomach and squirmed through the small gap.

When they were all safely inside the gate, they retrieved their belongings and hurried over to the tower. Alec and Jasmine began to climb the rickety wooden steps leading to the platform. Darius began to follow, then stopped.

Sammi, he thought.

She was at the bottom of the steps, her arms hugging her chest, looking up at the tower. Darius had forgotten about her fear of heights. Well, her fear of *falling from* heights.

No wonder she put up a fight when we got here.

"Come on, Sammi," Darius said. "They're looking for us. If we want to live, we need to start climbing."

"I can't," she said, shaking her head. "I'm too scared."

"We're *all* scared," Darius said. "But look what we've done. Your dad, he prepared you to survive. Take my hand." Darius held it out. "We'll climb together."

Seconds stretched to feel like minutes, like hours, like days as Darius waited for

Sammi. Finally, she slipped her hand into his. "OK," she said. "Let's survive."

Darius and Sammi took the steps side by side. As they climbed, he could feel Sammi start to shake. "Don't look down," he whispered. The wind swirled around them, making the lookout tower sway. It felt like the whole thing was about to topple over.

Jasmine and Alec had reached the platform and were out of sight. Darius guided Sammi up the last few steps.

"We made it," she whispered, collapsing onto the platform, lying flat on her stomach. Darius breathed a sigh of relief. If they stayed down and away from the edge, there was a good chance the Bigfoot wouldn't see them.

Faintly, Darius heard new cries from the monsters. They sounded angry, frustrated. *Good*, he thought.

They laid on the platform for almost an hour before the rain began again. It was not as fierce as the first storm. The platform's roof protected them from the downpour. Every so often, though, the wind would drive the rain sideways and the droplets would cut against them like needles. The tower continued to sway.

Sammi crawled over to Jasmine. They dug sleeping bags from their packs and hugged one another for warmth and safety and comfort. Jasmine reached out a hand to Alec, and he joined them.

Darius decided to risk a glance at the ground. He shimmied to the edge of the platform and slowly peered over it.

It was hard to see through the rain at first. But as his eyes adjusted, he spied several shapes near the clearing. They paced back and forth. One dragged its hand along the chain-link fence.

Thankfully, none of them looked up.

Darius retreated and joined the others.

The four Warriors, huddled together as one, waited for the terrifying night to pass.

CHAPTER TEN

Sunlight broke across the horizon and washed away the shadows. Darius peeled open his eyes. He felt as if he were living inside a dream. A familiar, welcoming sound drifted across the sky.

"Birds," he whispered.

Their chirps immediately put Darius at ease. It was the first time he'd noticed any wildlife since the group had encountered the moose drinking in the lake. That felt like centuries ago.

Darius unfurled from the others, who still

held each other in a tight knot under the comfort of their sleeping bags. Somehow, probably due to complete exhaustion, the other three were still sleeping. Darius crawled to the edge of the platform, apprehensive but no longer terrified, and peered over.

They were alone. There was nothing prowling the clearing. The Bigfoots were gone.

"Guys," he said, shaking the others awake. Slowly, their eyes fluttered open. They all looked at Darius expectantly. "I think it's safe to go down."

They carefully descended the lookout tower steps. Darius held Sammi's hand again, but it seemed her intense fear from the night before had been washed away with the rain.

After squeezing back through the gate, the quartet started the last leg of their hike towards the ranger station. The dread of losing Mr Horton still weighed heavily on them, but the further they walked in peace, the safer they felt. The Bigfoots had vanished, the daylight driving them back into hiding.

Like an oasis on a scorching desert day, the ranger station and trading post appeared at the end of the trail.

"We made it!" Alec cried out.

The Warriors quickened their pace, reaching the ranger station and bursting through the door. Darius couldn't believe how comforted he felt standing in the midst of the taxidermy weirdness. The owl. The moose. The deer and the leaping fish.

The door to the back office opened, and Ellis Malone emerged. She stopped, eyed the group of dirty, bloody teenagers, and asked, "What in the world happened to you?"

* * *

A helicopter thrummed overhead, and Darius craned his neck to look up at it. A blanket was wrapped around his shoulders. He and the other Warriors stood near the dock, where several boats – the Coast Guard, the Department of Natural Resources and the Police among them – had anchored. Jasmine sat on a bench near the ranger station. A paramedic knelt in front of her, attending to her knee. Cleaned of blood and in the light of day, the injury had turned deep purple with bruising. Darius had no clue how she'd managed to run through the woods the night before.

She's a real *Warrior,* he thought.

Ellis and her son, Ben, had heard the campers' terrified account from the night before. Ben had immediately called the police. The rangers did not seem to react the first time Darius and the others mentioned the word Bigfoot. But when the officers arrived at the ranger station from the mainland to question them, Ellis said, "The poor things must be delirious. They're rambling about make-believe creatures."

And so, when the police *did* hear their harrowing account, the group was met with disbelief. Darius even saw one of the officers smirk when Alec spoke of smashing the walking stick against the Bigfoot's chest.

Of course they don't believe us, he thought.

When Alec suggested they read the story in the book Jasmine had borrowed, he had searched his pack for it. It wasn't there. "I must have left it at the campsite when we packed up our things," he'd said sheepishly.

"We've had recent reports of bears," Ben said to one officer. "I discovered their den in a cave on the east side of the island earlier this summer."

"What?" Darius turned to Alec and whispered, "I thought they told us there weren't any bears?"

"They did," Alec replied. "At least, I . . . I think they did."

The officers appeared to believe Ben's story, that the kids had run into a large bear, that another bear had attacked Mr Horton and dragged him off to its den. The Wilderness Warriors knew the truth, though. It wasn't a bear that had taken Mr Horton.

"What about the Hendersons?" Darius asked Ellis.

She seemed puzzled. "What about them?"

"We found Mr Henderson's pack," he said. "We talked to Mrs Henderson on the walkie-talkie. She was scared and in danger."

Ellis Malone shook her head. "I'm not sure

what you mean," she said. "The Hendersons returned to the ranger station the afternoon before last and hired a private boat to return them to the mainland before the storm hit." She walked to the glass counter and retrieved a clipboard. Sure enough, on the visitor's log, there was a listing for a boat arrival and the departure time of Mr and Mrs Henderson. Their signatures were scribbled next to it.

"I don't understand," Darius said. "I talked to Mrs Henderson on the walkie-talkie. She told me to get help."

"What walkie-talkie?" an older officer with deep wrinkles and a thick moustache asked.

"I . . . I lost it," Darius replied.

The officer nodded, ran his tongue along the inside of one cheek. "Ya lost it, eh?"

Darius stayed silent.

A search party, including two helicopters

from the mainland, was sent out into the forest to look for Mr Horton. While the Warriors waited, the officers gave them food and blankets.

Darius looked up as the helicopter made another pass and Jasmine had her knee examined. Alec and Sammi stood together, waiting to hear news from the search party.

An hour passed before the walkie-talkies hooked to every officer's belt or shoulder harness crackled to life. "We've got him!" a voice shouted. "We have an adult male, discovered in a cave along the island's east shore. We're bringing him in."

Darius' heart swelled, and it felt like the weight on his chest had vanished. Sammi shed her blanket, rushing over and wrapping Alec in a hug. She even kissed him on the cheek. He instantly flushed red.

Soon after, one of the helicopters returned to the ranger station. It slowly lowered to the ground as officers backed the kids out of the way. Sand and dirt scattered as the pulsing wind from the rotors kicked it around. Darius shielded his eyes with one hand.

"Hop aboard!" the officer with the thick moustache bellowed at them. "We'll get you back to the mainland!"

He ushered the kids to the waiting helicopter and slid the rolling door open. Inside, a paramedic was hunched over a stretcher.

And on that stretcher, with a bloodied bandage around his head, was Mr Horton.

"Daddy!" Sammi burst into tears, leaping into the helicopter and draping herself over the stretcher.

Mr Horton reached one hand around her, holding her close. "Hey there, Warriors," he said weakly.

When the group was aboard, the officer

slid the helicopter door closed. The rotor noise became a loud hum as the chopper waited to lift off.

"What happened to you?" Sammi asked, touching the bandage.

Mr Horton shook his head. "I don't know," he said. His voice was weak and sounded like he'd been munching on gravel. "One minute I was going to sleep in my tent, the next I was waking up in a cave with two officers crouched over me."

"I'm so glad you're alive," Sammi told him, burying her head in his chest. She added in a muffled voice, "Wait until you hear what happened to us."

The helicopter slowly lifted off the ground. As they climbed into the sky, Darius pressed his forehead against the glass of the nearest window. He watched as Ellis, Ben and the remaining police officers and DNR officials milled about the ranger station.

Then he looked out at the island itself, at the needle-like pines jutting skywards, the water crashing along its rocky shoreline, the expanse of lake all around. It all looked so peaceful, so pristine.

As the helicopter soared over the island, Darius searched the forest and clearings for the Bigfoot.

They'd disappeared, hidden from sight.

Waiting, he thought, *for another group of unsuspecting hikers.*

EPILOGUE

Everyone had gone. The police officers making their reports. The DNR officials traipsing around. The helicopters hovering overhead. The kids and their guide, who was miraculously still alive.

All gone.

Finally.

Ellis rubbed at the scar on her forearm. It always seemed to itch nowadays. Today in particular. She sat down in one of the dusty, overstuffed chairs in the ranger station, resting her head back and sighing.

Ben entered the station. A canvas sack was slung over one shoulder.

"Did you get it all?" Ellis asked.

Ben nodded. "Everything I could find."

He walked to the coffee table, with its curled up doe and fawns inside, and upended the sack. Items tumbled out. Some were caked in dirt. Others were clean. The clumps of mud that spilled onto the table and floor didn't bother Ellis one bit. She had plenty of time to clean up now that everyone was gone.

Ellis eyed the items. A walkie-talkie. A shattered camera. A backpack. Everything they'd left, everything they'd lost.

"All traces of the Hendersons have been tidied up too," Ben said. "Like they were never here."

"Good thinking, making that fake entry on the visitor's log," Ellis said.

"Thank you, Mother."

Ellis picked through the belongings until she found what she wanted. Her book. It lay at the bottom of the pile, its cover curled and smudged with dirt. She had forgotten about it. It had been careless of her to keep the book out where it could be found.

Or, in this case, *stolen* by a nosy little brat.

"Good," Ellis said. She ran her hand over the book's cover. Then she stood and walked to her office.

No one was allowed in her office except Ben. A desk sat in the middle of the cluttered space. A bookshelf lined one wall, a display case the other. Ellis slid the book onto one of the shelves, then seated herself at the plush green desk chair.

In front of her on the desk was a sketchbook. One of the brats, the pretty one whose dad had booked the trip, owned a similar book. On the top page of the sketchbook was an ink drawing Ellis had just finished. A creature with long limbs, matted fur, and beady eyes stared off the page. Its eyes followed her every movement.

Behind her on the wall was a framed newspaper clipping. *WOMAN SURVIVES FREAK BEAR ATTACK!* the headline read. The black-and-white photo accompanying the story showed a young Ellis, eyes wild, clutching her bloody arm. Whenever she looked at the article, she regretted the first story she'd given reporters – the *true* story. The one published in the out-of-print book.

It was just easier to tell them it was a bear attack, she thought. Because it had given her time to recover. To plot out her future. To return to the island with her son.

"Do you think they bought it?" Ben asked, leaning against the door frame.

"Bought what?" Ellis asked.

"The story about the bears."

Ellis looked at the display case. There was only one thing inside it – the head of the snarling, angry beast that had attacked her so long ago. It bared its teeth, looking as menacing in death as it had when it was alive and hunting the forest around her. When she'd killed it, she'd earned the other monsters' respect. And as long as she kept bringing people to the island, like the ill-fated Hendersons or the pesky group of Wilderness Warriors, the creatures would continue to treat her as the leader of their pack.

"Of course they bought it," Ellis said with a smirk. "They always do. Because who'd believe in an island filled with Bigfoots?"

GLOSSARY

anonymous written, done or given by a person whose name is not known or made public

appalled shocked or horrified

beef jerky meat that has been cut into thin strips and dried

Bigfoot (also called Sasquatch) large, hairy, ape-like creature, supposedly found in north-western America

defiantly refusing to obey

devastation ruins, chaos or disorder caused by a violent action

lacerations deep cuts on the skin

mythical imaginary or not real

ominous something that gives the feeling that something bad will happen

outhouse outside toilet

peal loud sound or series of sounds

pleas extremely emotional requests

rustic simple, plain

secluded quiet and private

taxidermy preparing, stuffing and mounting skins of dead animals to make them look alive

thunderous producing a loud sound of or like thunder

trading post shop or other place where goods are bought and sold, usually in a remote area

urban legend story told as though it were true, although it usually isn't true or cannot be checked. It is often told as a funny story or a horror story.

DISCUSSION QUESTIONS

1. Darius isn't very excited about going on the trip at the start of the story. How have you adapted to a situation you didn't want to be in? Did you feel similar to how Darius felt?

2. Jasmine finds a book that talks about a Bigfoot attack. Were you able to guess who told the story? How do you think the story would be different if Jasmine hadn't found the book?

3. Imagine you are Sammi when her father goes missing. What would you do if you were in her situation? Talk about your decision using examples from the text.

WRITING PROMPTS

1. Darius and his friends have to outrun the Bigfoots during their time on the island. Imagine you're one of the Bigfoots. Write a scene from their perspective.

2. What are the early signs that something isn't quite right on Pine Island? Create a list of all the strange things about the island from your memory of the book.

3. Each character had a different viewpoint on their harrowing adventure. Pick one of the Wilderness Warriors and write a diary entry from their perspective about their trip to Pine Island.

ABOUT THE AUTHOR

Brandon Terrell has been a lifelong fan of all things spooky, scary and downright creepy. He is also the author of numerous children's books, including six volumes in the Tony Hawk's 900 Revolution series, several Sports Illustrated Kids graphic novels and a You Choose chapter book featuring Batman. When not hunched over his laptop writing, Brandon enjoys watching films (horror films especially!), reading, baseball and spending time with his wife and two children in Minnesota, USA.

ABOUT THE ILLUSTRATOR

Neil Evans lives on the south coast of the UK with his partner and their imaginary cat. Evans is a comic artist, illustrator and general all-around doodler of whatever nonsense pops into his head. He contributes regularly to the British underground comics scene, and he is currently writing and illustrating a number of graphic novels and picture book hybrids for older children.

PROOF PROVING DIFFICULT

The Bigfoot, also called Sasquatch, of this story is a cryptid. A cryptid is an animal we can't prove exists, even though we have many legends and stories about it. *Cryptid* comes from the Greek word for "hidden", and cryptozoology means "the study of hidden animals". Cryptozoology attempts to prove that creatures such as Bigfoot, the Loch Ness Monster, the Wolpertinger and even dinosaurs are living animals today.

Cryptozoology is a pseudoscience because there is no evidence that cryptids exist. This doesn't stop people from trying to find evidence, however. Since the 1960s, researchers and scientists have attempted to prove the existence of Bigfoot and other cryptids. They have studied footprints, looked at photographs and even seen video footage. But all of the evidence found so far is inconclusive at best or, at worst, a hoax.

Although being a cryptozoologist sounds like a life full of adventure, it can be hard and unrewarding work. Cryptozoologists are rarely paid to research and often have to look for physical evidence in places where vehicles can't go. This can mean getting plenty of exercise! And before doing that, they have to read about sightings and legends to know where to start looking. For instance, Bigfoot stories came from the Coast Salish people, who told stories of a "wild man". Because these Native Americans lived in the United States' Northwestern Pacific Coast, a cryptozoologist would want to start looking there. A beginner cryptozoologist might also consider pursuing a degree in zoology to better understand animal behaviour and be able to predict where cryptids would look for food and shelter.

Although Bigfoot remains a mystery, searching for unknown creatures has paid off in some cases. In the Ituri Forest of central Africa, around the 1900s, locals told stories of an unusual creature. It was short, had a tall neck, a long tongue and stripes! Scientists at one point thought it may have been a zebra. Imagine their surprise to find it was actually a new animal, a relative of the giraffe, called the okapi.

Cryptids come from fascinating stories that people love to hear. These stories inspire people to imagine seeing a cryptid for themselves one day. Today more of the world has been explored and documented than ever before, so there are fewer places for these creatures to hide. This means we may soon be able to prove whether Bigfoot is real or not, once and for all.

SPINE SHIVERS